Llama Unicorn Song

by

Toy Fan TV

illustrated by

visoeale & toy fan tv

with some images from creative fabrica

YOU'RE CUTE AND CUDDLY

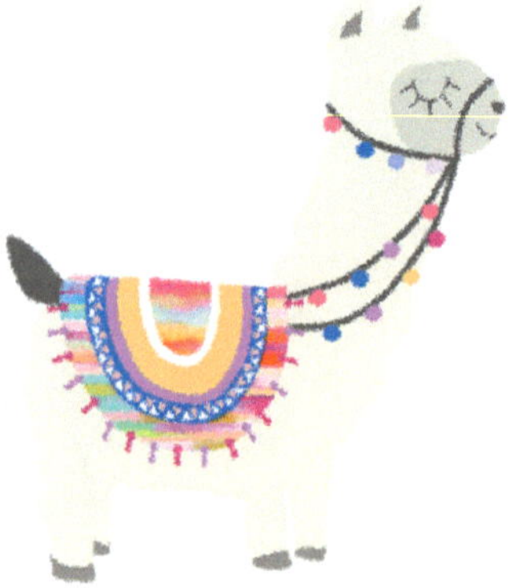

so soft and fluffy

Naturally adorable

Absolutely Magical!

Oh! My llama unicorn!

Oh! My llama unicorn!

you're sweet and dreamy

Sparkly and Rainbowy!

MaRVeLOUSLY MYThiCaL

wonderfully whimsical

Oh! My llama unicorn!

Oh! My Llama Unicorn!

www.ingramcontent.com/pod-product-compliance
Lightning Source LLC
Chambersburg PA
CBHW041611120626

46551CB00002B/401